Everything That Looks Good, Ain't Good for You!

a novel by

GWEN CANNON

G Publishing LLC
Detroit, Michigan

Edited by: Francene Ambrose Gunn
Cover Design: Brittany Janay Jackson
Published by G Publishing, LLC
P. O. Box 24374
Detroit, MI 48224

ISBN 13: 978-0-9801297-8-6
ISBN 10: 0-9801297-8-8

Library of Congress Control Number: 2007943504

Printed in the United States of America

Acknowledgements

First and foremost, I give praise and thanks to my creator because without His presence and guidance in placing the right people in my life to make this book happen, I could not have achieved this.

To my loving husband James, with his trademark statement to me when I was up many late nights pecking away on the computer. He would say, "Gone Ba, do the damn thing," Thank you baby!!

I would like to express a special thank you to my mother, the person who gave me life. My mother is a strong black woman who leaves a mark on anyone who meets her. I use her shoulder to cry on when nothing seems to be going right. She would always tell me, there's a reason for everything, God has a plan.

I love you Mom! Because, without her bringing me into this world, I know I couldn't have achieved this. With God, family and friends, I know there is no limit to what I can achieve.

Introduction

We go through life wishing, and wanting things we can't have. Things that look glamorous now, will be the same things that break you down to your knees. We jump into relationships without really getting to know that person. We have to stop looking at what's on the outside. No one knows what happens once the doors are closed. We wish, we pray and hope for better things. We even go out of our way trying to impress someone. We put on false faces in life to get what we want, and it doesn't matter who gets hurt in the process.

Growing up in the ghetto, I was faced with many obstacles that prevented me from doing what I wanted to do. I never tried to be someone I wasn't; my mother taught me to be strong, and not to be a follower. Those were words of advice that have followed me throughout my life.

As a person who came from the ghetto, I chose not to be a product of my environment. People treat you, the way you present yourself. If you act Ghetto-fabulous, you'll be treated in that manner. If you act with respect and dignity, people will treat you with respect. So to my beautiful brothers and sisters out there in the world, whether African American, Caucasian, Chinese, or Hispanic, don't look at the value of things, look at the value of life. Hold your head up high and say, "I can be whatever I want to be," So take control of your life, don't let the people in your life take control of you.

Hey, this is only the beginning!

Chapter - 1

Grace

It was Friday, our weekly girls night out looking for Mr. Right. Grace was on her usual mission, trying to find Mr. Right. Her version of Mr. Right, looking fine, and have a large cash flow. Well on this particular night, things would happen that would affect Grace for the rest of her life. I was dressed to impress, my hair was fly, nails manicured and toes pedicured to the max. Hey, what can I say? I was looking good; oh by the way, my name is Max.

I thought I'd share this little experience with you ladies, to let you know, there is a lesson to be learned when putting yourself out for a man. Don't think that he is the one and only. The one who you think will sweep you off your feet and take you to la-la land. Get a grip. It isn't a storybook ending; put that shit in the trash. Just always think about what your momma told you, "Everything done in the dark comes to light,"

My girl, Grace was one of those females that thought if she slept with you, put the shit on you right, you'd be hers for life. I'm always telling this girl, if you act like a hoe, the man is going to treat you like a hoe! Damn, don't this girl know shit about men?

Trust me, this went in one ear, and out the other. My motto was, "Always give the man something to think about; make him wonder what's up with you girl, make him want to get to know you, not just what's up under your clothes,"

Well, let me get back to this particular night. It was about 9:30 p.m. There was a cool breeze outside, perfect night to go out on the town. We decided to go to Club Red, the hottest spot in Detroit, known to be packed with fine men, carrying helluva cheddar. Grace, my home girl from kindergarten, always had this reputation of giving good head. Niggas was calling her deep throat and shit. I told her that shit ain't cute, no way in hell I want to have a reputation like that. If anything, give me a rep for being smart as hell, and taking care of business.

"Grace, Grace, you ready?" I said.

"Not yet, tell me which dress I should wear Max?" said Grace.

"Neither, they both make you look like a skank ass hoe!" I replied.

"Oh no, you didn't go there Max,"

"I'm not going to be fake with you Grace. That shit ain't cute. You look like a hoe!" I said.

"Well you pick out something then," "Ain't shit in your closet Grace, that I would want to wear," I said.

"I'll tell you what, we'll stop by my place, and grab something sexy, and sophisticated. I see now, I'm going to have to school your ass on what men like, and a deep throat bitch ain't it. Let me change that statement, men like a lady in the street, and a freak in the bed, so hold off on that deep throat shit for your man, not every nigga you meet," I said.

"Hell yeah, Max. That's what I'm talking about. That shit sound good as hell," said Grace.

"Ok, if it sounds so good, why the fuck you keep getting down on your knees with every nigga you meet?" I asked.

"I know I need to change my ways, but damn, I'm just trying to please a nigga," said Grace.

"Well, please them with your presence and grace. Ain't that your name? Grace. I don't know what I'm going to do with you girl. You got to stop thinking with what's between your legs, and use your brain. You would think you learned something in school," I said.

"Ok, ok, get the fuck off my back Max. Let's get back to picking me out something to wear, I don't need you up in here acting like you my momma."

"Grace, what do you think about this dress?"

"Max, that's too homely. What about that one, hanging up over there in the corner?"

"Oh hell naw, that was Tony's favorite dress," I said.

"Max your ass ain't even with Tony, so give up the damn dress," laughed Grace.

"Ain't no way in hell I'm letting you strut your stuff in that dress Grace, that's Dolce Gabbana. That dress cost me my pay check, and then some. I might decide to wear it to Club Red, then, we'll both have a reputation, as switching up outfits. Hell naw, no way.

You can wear that black halter dress. That should get you the attention you want, and you'll still look sophisticated, too. We gotta go shopping for you Grace. Maybe sometime next week, change your whole wardrobe," I said.

"I don't see shit wrong with my wardrobe Ms Max," said Grace.

"Ok Grace, I guess I have to break the shit down for you. For one, everything you wear looks like you glued the shit to your ass, or it looks like you put your little sister's shit on. Like I said, we need to go shopping for your ass. I see now, I have my work cut out for me. We're going to work on you, my sister, so we can trash that reputation you put on yourself," I said, shaking my head.

"And what reputation is that Max?" asked Grace.

"Don't stand there and act like your ghetto fabulous ass don't know. Ok Grace, tell me what the niggas be calling you? It ain't Grace. I know that for a fact. Let me guess, is it deep throat? I guess when you give six, or seven different niggas head, it spreads like wild fire. What did you think Grace? Oh, but as you put it, if I put the shit on them right, by the end of the night my purse will be full. That kind of thinking, will get your ass in trouble, you need to stop acting like a hoe," I said.

Chapter - 2

Grace

I hate to say it, but my girl really got played again as usual this night. I guess the shit we discussed earlier went right out the window, because as soon as we hit the door, she was her usual self, all up in every niggas face in the place, striving for the attention she so loved.

The music was bumping, and the club was packed to full capacity. I'm surprised someone didn't send the fire marshal's in. The usual drug dealers were hanging around the bar to see what pussy they could get with tonight. Been there, done that, that shit is scary as hell. I don't think I could do that drug dealer scene.

I ordered my favorite drink, a strawberry daiquiri, with whipped cream. I was enjoying the atmosphere. Damn, the DJ was tight. He put my jam on, *(damn too much booty in the pants).* I couldn't help myself, I went straight to the dance floor by myself and was shaking my ass like I owned the place.

I guess you can tell when a sister hasn't been out in a while. After my breakup with Tony, I just chilled with the club scene. I would go out every three, or four months, so I was overdue. I could see niggas, just standing around looking. I guess I was the entertainment, seeing that I was on the dance floor by myself. Next thing I know, this fine ass brother, walks up to me, and starts dancing with me.

I was like damn! Who made this pretty mother-fucker? Damn, he's fine. Listen ladies, I mean like wet between your legs fine, you know a nigga that you see, and your nipples start to tingle, and get hard. That's how fine this nigga was. We were grooving to the music, we were in our own world, I was dropping like it's hot, and shit.

"Damn girl, don't do me like that," he said.

"If you can't handle the heat, I suggest you step off," I said.

"Oh baby ain't no doubt I can handle all this and some," he said.

I started teasing the nigga. "I don't think you can handle all this ass. Listen to the song, too much booty in the pants," I said.

"You got that right, baby girl," He said.

"I'm not your baby girl, and the name is Max," I replied.

"Ok, ok, calm down pretty lady. A brother just wants to get to know you," he said.

I was really enjoying myself talking shit to this nigga, knowing ain't shit gone happen after the club. Grace always told me, I talk a lot of shit. I'd rather talk shit, than to be laying up on my back, or down on my knees.

I could see Grace standing next to this brother. She was watching us, the next thing I know, her ass comes strutting toward us, and starts dancing behind him. She was rubbing her ass up against him, and shit, I couldn't believe my girl was acting like this. I gave her a look, that said get the fuck on and get your own partner; this one is mine tonight. But she just kept on rubbing and grinding up against him.

Finally, I just walked off the dance floor, and let her get her groove on. I was so damn mad. I could have just busted her in her damn face. But instead of acting ghetto fabulous, I sat down and ordered me another drink, and chilled. I sat there watching her putting her, so called moves on him. I guess he was impressed because his hands were all over her ass, and shit. She wasn't saying nothing, but smiling in his face.

"Damn, that nigga tried to dance the fucking night away, my damn feet hurt. Max, I hope you're not mad? I couldn't help myself. That nigga is fine as hell, and he's going home with me tonight. Shit Max, I think I've found my husband," said Grace.

"I guess our earlier discussion didn't mean shit. Just like you Grace, and by the way who the hell wants to meet their future husband at a god damn club. Damn, you desperate as hell. You just said fuck me, and took over," I said.

"Ok, since you said it, fuck you Max," said Grace.

"Sorry Grace, I'll pass on that note, baby. I'm strictly dickly," I said.

"Max, I know you ain't trying to call me gay bitch," said Grace.

"You said it, I didn't," I said.

"Ok, let me rephrase that. I don't want to fuck you Max, but fuck you anyway," said Grace.

"Ok Grace, whatever floats your boat. I'm not going to swap insults with you tonight. I'm here to have a good time. It's been months since I've been out. I just want to enjoy myself," I said.

"Ok Max, I'm sorry. Let's get this party started!" as she started dancing.

Gwen Cannon

Chapter - 3

Grace

Just like Grace, like I said, fine as hell, and money, that's all she need to know. Well she did take Mr. Fine home, and of course she had to call me and brag about the explicit details of their little sex escapade. I told her that's a little too much information baby girl. I don't want to hear about how you got sucked, and fucked. Damn, it's been awhile for me, so I don't need to hear that shit.

"That shit you pulled last night Grace, coming out on the dance floor, and just taking over. That shit still got me pissed off. You didn't even give me a fucking chance to ask the nigga what was his name, and occupation. Your ass just jumped on in and snatched him up," I said.

"I can't help it if he liked what he saw Max," said Grace.

"Oh, don't get it twisted. He liked the fact that this bitch don't care if I'm rubbing all over her ass, that's what he liked. But you just can't see that shit. Anyway, you lucky you my girl, because I would have told your ass where to go, and where to get off, right there on the dance floor.

So tell me, what is Mr. Fine Ass' name, and what does he do for a living?" I asked.

"Huhmmmmm," said Grace.

"No, please tell me you got his government name Grace? Don't be going silent on me now. I told your ass, over and over again about that shit. That nigga could be a rapist, or murderer. Who knows what, and who else he been fucking with. How stupid can you be? Damn!" I said.

"We met up the next morning at IHOP," she had this big ass grin on her face.

"So what you all smiles about Grace?"

"I'm in love!" said Grace.

"In love with who? Joe blow, or John Doe?, you don't even know the nigga name," I said.

"Max, I have a confession to make, and don't go getting all big sister on me, and shit. I slipped up, and didn't use a condom with him,"

"Damn Grace, that's some foul shit. You let this nigga just go up in you raw? You don't even know him. Damn. You don't have any morals when it comes to your body. Your body is a temple, treat it like one. He could have anything, that shit be on the fucking news every day.

I don't know, why the hell I hang out with your dumb ass, triple – f," I said.

"Max, don't be calling me that shit," said Grace.

"If the shoe fits, your stupid ass wears it very well. I hope the niggas, don't be thinking I'm easy, 'cause I hang out with you," I said.

"I ain't easy Max," said Grace.

"Ok then, tell me what the fuck you call it. Yeah, I thought so. You ain't got shit to say now," I said.

"But Max, that nigga was too fine, and his pockets were full of cash," said Grace.

"How the fuck you know his pockets was full of cash? Did you get some of the cash? Or did you just get your pussy wet for free? A handsome face and a clean looking nigga don't make him fucking king of the castle for a night. But, as usual Grace, I know you fucked for free. That's why I call you triple – f.

Don't be looking all shocked and shit. The truth hurts, don't it? Maybe, that's what your ass needs--a fucking reality check. Maybe you need to hear the fucking truth sometimes. I try telling you shit, but it really don't fucking matter. I wouldn't say shit to you, if I didn't care Grace. I know you don't like what I'm saying by the look on your face. Grace, I love you like a sister, and you got to stop jumping into bed with every nigga you meet. Have some respect for yourself, as well as your body. If you don't respect yourself, who will? My mama always told me to walk with my head high, and demand the respect I deserve. Men can read into a woman. It's all about how you carry yourself. You are too pretty, and smart to just settle for every man that looks good, and that you think has a big cash flow," I said.

Grace wasn't trying, to hear shit I was saying. It was like this nigga had her mesmerized or something. Shit, I think it was the other way around, from the looks of it. I think the nigga put it on her.

"Grace, are you listening to what I'm saying? Grace, you need to take your ass to the doctor, and get checked out. He could have AIDS, STDs, and who knows what else. Did he give you his number? Oh yeah, you gave him yours, right? I should have known, brother probably told you he didn't have a home phone, just hit him up on his cell. Did you at least get his government name to go with the number?

Remember, the nigga had a pocket full of money. I guess it's going to take something drastic to get through your fucking head. You don't believe shit stank!" I said.

Max, don't be fucking playa hating," said Grace.

"Playa hating, shit if that's what you want to call it. Bitch, I'm just trying to get you to realize that fucking every nigga you meet, ain't shit cute, or sexy about it. Oh, but I forgot who I was talking to. Ms "I'm gone put it on the nigga." Trust me Grace, you are going to regret that shit one day. I swear on my fucking brother's grave, you are going to regret it. And remember, Max told you so," I said.

Chapter - 4

Lynn

"Lynn, what's taking you so long? We gotta go. I don't want to be late. Damn, I thought Mya was slow. Your ass got her beat," I said.

"Max, I'm coming, damn!" said Lynn.

Lynn is my little sister, one of them broads who always seems to think she's god's gift to men. I can remember when we were growing up, her ass stayed in front of a mirror--always, brushing her hair, and shit, making faces. I guess she was trying to see what expression she should use on a nigga. When weaves came out, oh my sister lost her fucking mind. I think she thought that shit was really her damn hair.

I used to tell her, "Damn, who made you queen of the fucking day. That shit in your head ain't yours. It came off some horse's ass,"

I remember how we used to argue over the bathroom. I used to tell my mother we need two damn bathrooms. Ms Diva would get in there for at least thirty minutes just to put on make-up. Now that was fucking ridiculous. Who needs, thirty minutes to make up their face? When it came to men--that was another issue. She actually thought a nigga was supposed to bow down to her. You might be laughing, but I'm fucking serious.

Let me tell you about one of her many escapades. It was Wednesday, I remember, because we always went to Chili's for their Wednesday special. We were in the parking lot. This brother came up to us and starting in on Lynn, telling her, how sexy she was.

Of course, she was feeding into all this. She loves when a nigga tells her how cute and sexy she is. Before I know it, Lynn ass tells this nigga, "Prove how sexy I am to you; kiss my feet."

Do you know this dumb ass nigga, got down on all fours, and kissed her fucking feet? I just burst out laughing, I told him you must be fucking desperate as hell, to kiss somebody's feet you just met. Don't get me wrong, I love for a nigga to suck my toes. But a total stranger, naww! I dragged her ass out of that parking lot before this nigga started sucking on some-thing else.

Now that we're older, my sister still hasn't changed her Diva ways. I can't for the life of me figure out how she got that way. I guess you could say, it came from niggas, always telling her how fucking cute she was.

Yeah my little sis is cute, but she should realize that the world does not revolve around her. She needs to get a fucking grip, and realize she is not the universe. I guess that's why every man she meets only sticks around for a hot second; she's stuck on herself.

I remember the day she met Corey Smith, her daughter's father. Nice, handsome brother. We were at Fairlane Mall. Lynn was in her usual mode, Ms Diva. Corey came up to Lynn with a weak ass line telling her she must be heaven cause looking at her he knows he must have just died. I just broke down laughing so hard. I thought the shit was cute though. Lynn just smiled and tried to play hard to get, as usual.

Come to find out, Corey had a degree in Business Management, and was working for General Motors. Now that's what I'm talking about--a legal nine-to-five job. He was very respectful, and seemed to know how to treat a lady. I talked Lynn into giving him her number. I told her, you never know, he might be your husband one day. Give the brother a chance. Corey wined and dined Lynn and gave her whatever she asked for. Corey was head-over-heels in love. I knew just by the way he would look at Lynn, like she was the only one in the room.

Now that's what I call love. Every other month Lynn and Corey were flying off to some exotic island.

"Damn, I'm jealous Lynn. Next thing you know you gone be telling me y'all about to get married. What the hell do y'all be doing on those islands?" I asked.

"Ask Corey. He always ends up leaving me shopping by myself for at least two to three hours. I don't know what the fuck he could be doing on a strange island we never been to. Max, I need to talk to you about something," said Lynn.

"What's up baby sis?"

"I think I might be pregnant," said Lynn. "Oh, hell naw. Are you sure? Did you talk to Corey about this?" I asked surprised.

"You're the first person I have mentioned this to."

"Lynn, I think you should go get checked out by a doctor first before, you make any real decisions," I said.

"I'm not trying to be tied down with a baby Max,"

"Lynn, maybe you should think about it first. Let's go get you a pregnancy test," I said. Well, the results were positive, and Lynn was pregnant.

"So, when are you going to tell Corey?" I asked.

"Corey doesn't have to know. I'm getting an abortion."

"Lynn, please don't make such a drastic decision now. Please take time to think this through, and at least tell Corey," I said.

"I already know what he's going to say Max. That's all he talks about is having a baby," said Lynn.

"Well, can you blame the man? He's not getting any younger, why wait. He's got a damn good job, he's stable, and I can tell he loves kids," I said.

Lynn wasn't trying to hear shit I was saying. She wanted to have an abortion. I finally convinced Lynn to tell Corey. As I guessed, he was excited, and happy. Somehow, Corey talked Lynn into having the baby. I just wonder what he said to convince her.

"Max, I want you to go with me and Corey for my doctor's appointment."

"I thought you would never ask. Thank you so much Lynn for making me a part of your special moment. Hey, I'm going to be an auntie," I said.

"Don't start that mushy shit Max," said Lynn. "Hey, I'm excited. I don't know about you. When are you going to tell the soon-to-be grandma and grandpa?" I asked.

"As soon as we leave the doctor's office," said Lynn.

"Lynn, mom is going to be so excited. She's always asking me when am I going to make her a grandma? Thanks Lynn, you saved me," I said.

"Fuck you Max! You're not the one who's going to be walking around with a big ass belly," screamed Lynn.

"Don't worry Ms Diva; you'll get your shape back." I couldn't help but laugh.

"You damn right, I am. I'm going to be on the treadmill every fucking day after I have the baby. Well, I hope everybody is fucking happy, because right now, I am depressed as hell," said Lynn.

"Aaaw, that's just your hormones talking. Wait until you look into your beautiful baby's eyes. You're going to fall in love. So, Lynn, tell me, what did Corey say to you? I know he had to promise you something for you to agree to have this baby," I said.

"Max, you think you know everything," said Lynn.

"Well, am I right? What did he promise you? A ten carat ring? A mansion? Come on Lynn, tell me," I begged.

"Ok, Max, but promise you won't be mad."

"Lynn, what the fuck did you do?"

"Max, Corey said that he would take full custody of the baby, and he promised to give me $100 thousand," smiled Lynn.

"Are you out of your fucking mind? I just started crying, the tears would not stop. Lynn, how could you just sell off your own flesh and blood as if it were a piece of jewelry? I knew you were selfish, but this shit takes the cake," I shouted.

"Max, don't be going all political on me. You would have done the same thing. You know if someone offered you that type of money, you would not refuse," said Lynn.

"That's where you're wrong little sister. I have morals and beliefs, and selling off my child is not one of them. Don't you love Corey? Or is it his money?" I asked.

"Money talks, bullshit walks," as the saying goes. I see you're all upset Max. I'll talk to you later," said Lynn, as she walked off.

After my conversation with Lynn I didn't know what to do. Should I tell our mother? I was totally lost for words. I called Corey the next day and he confirmed what Lynn had stated. It didn't seem to bother Corey that she was actually going to take money from him for their child. He just said, "Max, you know your sister. She loves m-o-n-e-y! I knew when I offered her that money, she wouldn't get an abortion. Even through all this, I still love your sister. I guess love is blind."

Everyone was all excited, when they found out about Lynn's pregnancy. Everyone wanted to be in on the baby shower, including Grace who's always crying, broke. Nine months went by quickly. Before I knew it, little Gina Simone Smith was born April 19, 2007, weighing 7 pounds, one ounce.

I couldn't believe how emotional I was during the delivery. It was a beautiful experience. I'm still in shock that Lynn actually signed full custody to Corey even after she saw this beautiful baby. I cried so hard that day, not only for my niece, but also for God to forgive my sister for doing such a cruel thing. My mother and father didn't know about the agreement until Gina was born. My mother let Lynn have it full blast. I can't remember the last time I heard my mother use such foul language, not since, she got saved.

It still puzzles me how she could look at such a beautiful baby and just give her away. Corey being the kind person he was, made sure me, and my mother got to see Gina as much as possible. I wasn't hurt by the fact that Corey had full custody. He's an excellent father and role model. It's just that I don't know what is wrong with my sister.

She kept saying that she didn't want to be tied down to a crying baby, that she was too young. Lynn did make sure Gina was dressed like a little angel, so she did all of Gina's shopping for Corey, but she refused to take back custody of her daughter. She would always say, as long as she knows who her mother is, she's alright. Her excuse was, there were too many things going on in her life right now to be tied down with a baby. Corey was handling a little infant, what was her excuse? I still don't understand why Corey was still putting up with Lynn.

Chapter – 5

Mya

"Hey girl what's up," I said.

This is my girl Mya, always fly as hell, wearing the latest designner clothes. "Ms Materialistic" is what I call her, and a money chaser. What I don't understand about Mya, is that the girl got it going on. She has two degrees. You heard me right the first time. Like I said, my girl has two degrees. Smart as hell, got a good ass job, has always held her own. But when it came to a nigga, Mya always had to have a thug. I think the shit turned her on, or something. She could have any nigga she wanted, but she always preferred the hardcore street nigga.

What these niggas didn't know was they always thought they were getting this smart ass, college woman who didn't know shit about the street life. Thinking they can just pull any kind of shit over on her. Little did they know, Mya was straight off the block ghetto fabulous. Oh, when it was time for business she would put on her business face; when it was time for the streets, home girl's whole attitude changed. Like I said if you didn't know her, you would never know what hit you.

Niggas thought they could pull whatever game on her they wanted, but little did they know, Mya was straight from the hood. Mya was what you would call a true diva, not like my little sister Lynn. Lynn could take some lessons from Mya, regarding what Diva status is. Mya hated when I would call her Diva; she always preferred the name Cutie. Hey, just call her cell, she'll answer by saying, "This is cutie."

Mya got the reputation for being a gold digger, totally different from my girl Grace. Grace would give up the pussy at the drop of a dime if she thought the nigga had any type of paper.

I guess Mya's anthem song would be, *She ain't nothing but a gold digger," by Kanye West, and Jamie Foxx.* Every time we would be at the club and the DJ played her song, Mya was on the floor doing her national gold digger anthem dance. That shit used to be funny as hell. Whatever Mya was doing to the niggas, it kept them coming back for more. I asked her one day.

"Damn girl, tell me your secret, do you be deep throating a nigga? Doing some kind, of gymnastic shit on them," I said.

She used to laugh at me saying it was her little secret.

"Like you said Max, never tell what goes on behind closed doors with you, and your man," said Mya.

"Whatever bitch!" I said. I couldn't hate on my girl, shit I just wanted to know what was her secret? Shit, put a sister on. Whatever my girl was doing, it worked because the niggas would be hooked. I think that shit turned them on, thinking she was this Ms Goody Two-Shoes, a book worm. They say niggas like a lady in the streets, and a freak in the bed. I guess the saying is true.

Mya's grandmother, Mrs. Mae, raised Mya ever since she was six months old. Mrs. Mae got legal custody of Mya. Mya's, mother was smart as hell, but when it came to drugs, getting high was her main priority. Mrs. Mae lived in the Jefferies Housing Projects, in Detroit, MI. She paid Mya's way through college by running street numbers (now that's what I call a true granny). Shit, she was a damn hustler for real. Everybody in the hood knew Mrs. Mae, was sweet as a button, would feed the needy, give you her last, but didn't take no shit. She would whoop a nigga's ass in a heartbeat.

She used to beat the shit out of her boy friend. This nigga was bigger than her, but that shit didn't stop Mrs. Mae.

I remember when her grand kids used to try to run up in the house. They would be getting chased home from school. Shit, Mrs. Mae would lock the screen door and tell them if you come in here, I'm gone whoop your ass for running, or you can put a whooping on them. They always took their chances and stayed outside, and fought their battles.

Living in the projects, you didn't have a choice, trust me I know. I can remember many days when I had to whoop a bitch's ass. Ghetto project chick is what Tony used to call me, but he loved this project chick. I got the reputation for being quiet, but would not hesitate about whooping your ass. Niggas used to say, "Don't mess with Max. Shit she will beat your ass down.

"Mya, bring your ass on, you the slowest person I know besides my sister Lynn. It takes you two fucking hours to get dressed, and don't talk about when we be getting ready to go to the club. You take all damn day," I said. "Fuck you Max," said Mya.

"You know what Mya, I'm tired of you, and Grace saying that 'fuck you Max', shit to me. I can't stand that shit," I said.

"Ok, Ms Sensitive, I'm going to come up with something different for your ass. And don't be fucking comparing me to Grace's hoe-ish ass," said Mya.

"Oh yeah, I have to apologize on that one. Grace is a hoe, and you are a sack chaser," I said.

"Ain't nothing wrong with chasing the almighty dollar," replied Mya, smiling.

"Oh yeah Mya, I forgot to tell you about what your girl Grace did to me at the club. Do you know she slept with this nigga the other night? Straight up raw. She had just met him at the club. To top it off, her hoe-ish ass snatched him up off the dance floor from me," I said.

"I know you ain't surprised Max. Shit we both know Grace don't give a fuck. If the nigga's cute, look like he got money, she don't give a fuuuucccckkkkkk,"

"Your ass is crazy as hell Mya. You're Ms Comedian."

"Hey like you always said Max, if the shoe fits, wear it, and Grace is wearing the shit out of it. I don't know why you trusted her around Tony when you were with him. That's why I didn't even attempt to introduce her ass to my friend when I bumped into her at the mall," said Mya.

"Oh yeah, she was telling me about that. She said she ran into you at Gino's Sports Wear. She said you just waved, and kept walking with this cutie you was with. She said you didn't even try to introduce her to him," I said.

"And I wasn't trying to. That's my girl, but I like I said, I just don't trust her ass. Too needy, always needing that extra attention," said Mya.

"I'm just afraid, she's going to end up with some shit she can't shake, know what I'm saying?" I said.

"I hear you Max, but she's a grown ass woman, and she needs to start taking responsibility for her stupid ass actions when it comes to men."

"Still Mya, she's our girl."

"I know that Max, but right is right, and wrong is wrong."

"Maybe you can give her some advice on men Mya. I been trying, and that shit go out with the wind, just like at the club the other night," I said.

"Face it Max, the bitch gone have to get a serious wake up call. I'm tired of talking about Grace. Let's hit the mall. I saw this cute two-piece I want to wear to RJ's concert Saturday," said Mya.

"Ooohhh Mya, you got tickets for that. Shit you must got some serious connects.

I stood in a long ass line the same day they went on sale, and the only seats available were balcony seats. Shit I'm trying to be up front and personal. I don't care what they say about my boy, he's still tight. What baller, you going with Mya?" I asked.

"Andre!

"Oh, you must really like Andre, because you normally kick a nigga to the curb after date number three. What is this date number five? You know I have a nickname for you, TSB," I said.

"And what does that suppose to mean Max?"

"Three Strike Bitch. If you ain't impressed by date number three, your ass know you be kicking a nigga to the curb."

"Ok, ok you got me Max. Damn, I be telling your ass too much shit about me. You got my MO down."

"Mya, when are you going to settle down with just one nigga? You know you getting old."

"Fuck you Max, and I ain't saying forget you. That shit don't sound right."

"You know I hate that shit, don't be saying fuck me," I said.

"Ok, bump you Max," said Mya.

"What the hell is bump you? You might as well go ahead and say fuck you Max. Mya it's killing you not to say fuck you. Ok Mya, you have my permission to say, fuck you Max," I said.

"Fuck you Max, fuck you, fuck you, fuck youuuuuuuuu! Damn that felt good,"yelled Mya.

"Shit, I hope so. You said the shit enough," I said.

Chapter – 6

Mya

"Mya, why don't you see if you can get me a couple of tickets to the concert? I know your ass probably got front row seats. Don't be smiling, I knew your ass did. Hook your sister up," I said.

"Max, only if you are taking my boy Tony," said Mya.

"Oh, hell naw Mya," I laughed.

"You know you still got mad love for Tony," Mya smiled.

"Honestly, I do. But he just broke it off with me with some sorry ass excuse. I thought we were soul mates. The sex was, oh my God I'm not even going to go there. But we got along so good I don't know what happened. He just changed.

I go home breaking shit so that I have a reason to call him to come over and fix it," I said.

"Max, that's some crazy shit," said Mya. "Love makes you crazy Mya," I said.

"Now you know why I haven't settled down Max. That shit you be telling me, I don't want to get hurt like that. A nigga just breaking it off with some sorry ass excuse, as you put it. So you can call me TSB all you want," said Mya.

"There must be something special about this Andre. What he do to you? I already know he had to spend mega paper just to get your phone number," I said.

"I guess you could say he's growing on me. He's like this cute little cuddly teddy. I can't let my guard down, got to stay at the top of my game. Before we hit the mall, I need to stop by my grandma's house," Mya said.

"Please don't let your bad ass cousin and his mother be over there. Last time I was over there, his little bad ass tried to hit up on me and shit," I said.

"Stop it Max, Rich is only ten," Mya said. "But the little nigga acts like he twenty-five. Shit he was spitting more game to me than the average nigga. Telling me, what he could do for me. I think his little ass was reincarnated," I said.

"Shit, I think that's an old man trapped in a ten year old body," said Mya.

"Shit Mya, he was putting street numbers in with your grandma the last time I was over there. I thought the little nigga was playing. He wrote a list and gave them to your grandma. Shit, she said Rich got a keep in ticket with her," I said laughing.

If you don't know what a keep in ticket is, it's a ticket with a list of numbers, that don't change, and they stay in with the number lady for a week, or until you tell her to stop playing them.

"Yeah Max, I have to say, Rich is different, I caught his little ass with a pack of condoms in his pocket. That shit was funny as hell. He said he be getting his groove on," said Mya.

"Shit Mya, I believe him. I'm not even going to repeat what he was saying to me," I said.

"If that was our girl Grace, shit I think she would have gave the little nigga some pussy," said Mya.

"Ooohhh, you wrong Mya. I know she will trick with any nigga with cash, but a ten year old," I said.

"Hey, I don't put nothing past your girl, she's a hoe," Said Mya.

"Hey, Mrs. Mae, ooohhh what you cookin'? That smells good," I asked.

"Greens, macaroni and cheese, candied yams, corn bread, and fried chicken," Ms Mae said.

"Max, come on with your greedy ass. Grandma did you see a blue bag I left in your bedroom closet yesterday?" asked Mya.

"Look in the hall closet Mya, I put it in there. Your nosey ass aunt was over here looking through it," Said Ms Mae.

"Aw shit, my shit better be in this bag," said Mya.

"What was in there Mya?" asked Max.

"The shit is gone. Andre had given me a bundle of cash to take home to count for him, and my crazy ass rushed out of here and left the shit. I don't know what the fuck I was thinking about. Grandma, call Roz and tell her to come over here. Don't tell her I'm here," said Mya.

"What's going on Mya?" asked Ms Mae.

"Grandma, please just call Roz, ok," said Mya.

"What you looking all happy about Roz?" asked Ms Mae.

"Nothing. What's up, ma? Is Rich over here?" asked Roz.

"Naw, Mya's looking for you," said Ms Mae.

"What did she say mama?"asked Roz.

"Roz, what's going on?" asked Ms Mae.

"Oh, what's up Mya?" asked Roz.

"You know what the fuck is up, excuse me grandma," said Mya.

"I didn't take nothing," said Roz.

"Who said you took something?" said Mya.

"I'm just saying, y'all always accusing me of something," said Roz.

"Roz, I'm only going to ask you one fucking time, where is my shit," asked Mya.

"Mya, I'll pay you back, I promise," said Roz.

"If you don't go get my fuckin' shit right now, I'm gone kill your ass. Don't fuck with me Roz," screamed Mya.

"Ok, ok, I got a little left over," said Roz.

"What the fuck you mean, a little left over? I want all my fucking money. Empty your fuckin' pockets now," hollered Mya.

"This is all I got," said Roz.

"Fifteen hundred dollars, how much did you fucking spend?" asked Mya.

"I don't know, I wasn't keeping count," said Roz.

"Shit, I guess the fuck you wasn't keeping count 'cause my shit is gone. Damn, this is fucked up," said Mya.

"Mya, do you know how much was in the bag?' asked Max

"Max I didn't even count the shit. Fuck, I need to call Andre, and play the shit off. I need to find out, how much money was in that bag. I know he doesn't know exactly how much, but shit, I need to have some clue as to how much. Roz lucky my grandma was here. I was going to fuck her up. Shit, I can't believe this happened. I don't know why the hell grandma took the damn bag out of her closet and put the shit in the hall closet. Let me call Andre.

"What's up boo?" asked Mya.

"Hey Mya, ready for tonight?" said Andre.

"Yeah!" replied Mya.

"Hey boo, how much money do you want me to deposit for you?" asked Mya.

"Three thousand, and bring the other thousand with you tonight," he said.

"I can't believe this shit. Now I have to come up off $2,500 of my own fucking money to cover this shit. That bitch gone pay me back every last fucking penny even if I have to take it out on her ass," shouted Mya.

"Damn, Mya, I'm sorry that shit happened," said Max.

"Max, I'm straight. I guess that's what I get for chasing the almighty dollar. I'm giving back money I took from one dope man, to give to another. Lesson learned, that shit I did in the dark, came right back at my ass," said Mya.

Chapter – 7

Mya

"Damn Max, I still can't believe I had to come up out of twenty-five hundred dollars," said Mya.

"Just be thankful you had the shit to replace. Ain't no telling what Andre would have done to your ass," I said.

"Andre wouldn't have done shit. Ain't no nigga gone put his motherfuckin' hands on me, believe that," said Mya.

"I'm just saying, Mya you don't know how that shit could have turned out. I guess the mall is out of the question now," I said.

"Hell naw, I'm still going to get me a fly ass outfit," Mya said.

"That's my girl. Don't shit hold you down.

I know your ass probably got a serious ass stash somewhere," I said.

"You know it. Gotta save for a rainy day, because they say when it rains, it pours. I just want to have my ass covered. You should always have at least six months worth of savings to cover all your bills, in case of an emergency. Shit my job might decide to fire my ass, you never know," said Mya.

"Damn Mya, I have to give you props, your ass be covering all avenues. Please school your girl Grace. If she used her brain instead of her body all the damn time, maybe she would have graduated from college. Who do you know stops going to college, with six months left before graduation," I said.

"Your girl, Grace! Damn, the Lodge freeway is backed up. I wonder what's going on," said Mya.

"Maybe it was an accident or something," I said.

"I don't know, but I'm about to get off; this is so irritating. You know I get fucking road rage. Oh, it's starting to move. So Max, what you gone do about you and Tony?" asked Mya.

"I don't know Mya. He's such a sweetheart. I know he wants to get back with me. When he's at my place fixing something, he always asks if I'm dating anyone," I said.

"And your answer is?" replied Mya.

"Shut up Mya, you know I can't just act like I be sitting around waiting on him. I play the shit off, make up some bogus ass name that I'm dating," I said.

"Hey, do what you gotta do," replied Mya. "You straight on that shit with Andre?" I asked.

"Yeah, but my aunt gone pay that shit back, and some. She is crazy as hell. I'm surprised her ass didn't get locked up in Northville, you know that crazy house," said Mya.

"I can remember the day you introduced me to her. I said hello and your aunt just up and said, 'Oh, you one of them stuck up bitches like Mya.' I couldn't do nothing but laugh. You had already warned me about her. But the next day when I saw your aunt Roz, she asked me would I give her a ride to the store, like ain't shit happened. I was like damn, did she forget what she said to me yesterday?

You know I had to call her out Mya. I said you just called me a bitch yesterday, and now you want a ride. Can you believe your aunt said, "You still a bitch, I just want a ride to the store," I said.

"Sorry Max, I told you she was crazy," replied Mya.

"Mya, I don't want to meet no more of your crazy ass family members," I said.

"You got to meet the rest of the family. Grandma has a total of seven kids, five girls, and two boys," said Mya.

"Oh hell naw, that's too many. They all might be crazy," I said.

Chapter – 8

Grace

"Grace, have you heard from Mr. Fine Ass Big Money Baller? Don't look at me like that. I just asked you a question bitch," I said.

"Don't even go there Max," she replied.

"Why you acting all bitchy with me? I'm not the one who fucked the shit out of you, and haven't called," I said as I turned up my nose. I had to rub the shit in my girl's face, seeing that she practically stole the nigga off the dance floor from me that night. I haven't forgotten about that shit.

"Max please, I don't need that shit right now. I'm fucking behind in my bills, I don't have shit to eat in my refrigerator, and the last thing I need is you all over me talking about some motherfucker we met at the club," replied Grace sarcastically.

"Damn, Grace don't take it out on me. I didn't know you were having money problems. Do you need to borrow some money?" I asked.

"Naw, I should be ok. My unemployment check should be in the mail today," she replied.

"Damn, you haven't found a job yet?" I asked.

"Naw, it's tight out here now; nobody's hiring," said Grace as she walked into the living room.

"Grace, you been unemployed for four months. I know there's something out there. Shit, try the mall, they're always hiring," I shouted.

"Hell naw, I don't need you, and Mya coming in the store trying to get a discount on my ass," said Grace.

"That's what friends are forrrrr!" sang Max.

"Don't be singing that shit--it ain't funny," said Grace.

"Grace you should take your ass back to school and finish up your degree. I don't know why your ass dropped out when you only had six more months to go. Oh now I remember, the other fine ass nigga that promised you the world, took you to Las Vegas, and dropped your ass after you got back home. Never, ever let a nigga stop you from enhancing your knowledge to do better in life. You should always put God first, then yourself, and the niggas feelings last. You got to do what's right for Grace. Don't be out there trying to please every nigga you meet," I said.

"Max, I don't need you up in here trying to play momma; I got one," said Grace.

"Ok, ok, I'm just trying to look out for my girl. You know I got your back no matter what. But, I don't care what you say, I'm going to keep on hounding your ass until you go back, and finish school. Ok, I'm sorry. Don't be looking all depressed and shit. You wanna go to the movies or out to eat?" I said.

"Naw, I don't have any money to be doing no extra shit," replied Grace.

"Well I'm out. I'll call you later Grace." I said.

I decided to go to the mall. I wasn't the type to be sitting all lonely and shit in a movie theatre. I think I'll stop at *Limited Express*, my favorite store. Oh, my God, guess who walks in with some raggedy ass, dime store looking hoe all over him. You guessed right, Mr. Fine

Ass Big Money Baller. I didn't know if he would remember me from the club, so I just walked over to the counter. He was standing next to the cash register, so I played it off, and asked the sales lady if the halters were going on sale.

You wouldn't believe this shit, but this sorry ass nigga started trying to hit on me. So I played along with the shit.

"Didn't you just come in with your woman?" I said.

"Naw, that's just a friend," he replied.

"Do I look familiar to you?" I asked.

"With a body, and face like that, shittt a nigga couldn't possibly forget your fine ass." He smiled.

I couldn't even hold the shit in; I just up and called his sorry ass out.

"Remember Grace, from Club Red, the one you went home with about a month ago, and fucked, and ain't called a sister since. That was my friend. That's what I say about y'all sorry ass motherfuckers," I screamed.

His so-called friend came out of the dressing room asking him, "What's going on baby?"

Do you believe this nigga had the audacity, to tell her, "This broad mad cause a nigga won't holla at her."

"Holla, motherfucker you got the wrong one today. You couldn't pay my ass to holla at you if you were the last motherfucker on earth. Sorry ass, hoe," I said.

The sales lady came up.

"Miss, miss, you have to leave the store, or I'm gonna have to call security," she stated as calmly as she could.

I was calling him every name in the book, but the child of God. Of course, I was escorted out of the store. I couldn't wait to get home, and call Grace and tell her about this lying motherfucker.

"Grace, pick up the goddamn phone. I know your ass probably over there screening your damn calls. Pick up," I said.

"Hello, this is Grace, what do you want Max? I don't feel like talking right now. I have a lot on my mind," said Grace.

"Grace what's up?"I asked.

But she wasn't saying anything.

"Hello, helloooo, Grace are you there?" I asked again.

Grace just started crying.

"What's wrong girl? You know you can tell me, are you sick? I can come over if you want me to," I said gripping the phone tightly.

I will never forget those words that came out of her mouth. Till this day that shit still gives me a knot in my stomach.

"Max, I got AIDS."

"That motherfucker gave me AIDS. Max what am I going to do? What am I going to do?' She tearfully asked.

I was speechless. I didn't know what the fuck to say. Before I knew it, I was speeding down the Lodge freeway on my way to Grace's apartment. I almost broke my hand, banging on her door.

"Grace, open the damn door. Damn, Grace are you sure he gave that shit to you? Because you've been sleeping with a lot of niggas," I said.

"Oh, so what are you saying Max? That I'm a hoe," said Grace.

She started crying again.

"You said it, I didn't," I replied.

"Some friend you are Max," she said.

"Grace, I am your friend. I'm just saying are you sure? This is some serious shit to be accusing someone of. You need to check all your sources, oops I mean whomever you have slept with in the last ten years. They say that shit can sneak up on you all the way back to ten years.

Ok this is what we are going to do. We are going to make a list of names that you can remember from the last ten years," I said.

I don't know if it was me, but Grace gave me this look of shock, like she didn't want to name every nigga that she had slept with.

"Grace, what's wrong? Just write a list, and we'll call every name, and tell them they need to go get tested," I said.

Grace just sat there in a daze.

"Grace is there more to this than you're telling me? I asked.

"Sit down Max. You know I love you like a sister, and you have always had my back, no matter what. But since this shit has happened, I have to tell you something that I know might change our friendship," said Grace.

"Ok, Grace, now you are scaring me. What the fuck is going on?" I asked.

"I have to tell you the truth. This has been hanging over my head for a while. I should have said something when it happened," said Grace.

By now I'm sitting down, wondering what the fuck could be so damn serious, that Grace is telling me that it might change our friendship.

"Ok Grace, tell me what the fuck happened that might change our friendship," I jumped up from the couch.

"I know this is going to hurt you Max, I'm scared to tell you, but I have to," Grace said tearfully.

"Look Grace, I'm on fucking pins, and needles. Tell me what the fuck is going on." I crossed my arms over my chest, and started patting my feet on the floor.

The next words to come out of Grace's mouth left me fucking speechless and numb as hell.

"I slept with Tony about a year ago."

Chapter - 9

Grace

Y ou talking about jaw dropping shock, I was fucked up, hearing those words come out of Grace's mouth. All I could do was get up, and head for the door. I know I had to be in the fucking twilight zone. My mind kept telling me, this can't be true, not my home girl, my sister for life. She wouldn't do no foul shit like that to me.

"Max, Max don't go! Please Max, let me explain," cried Grace.

Why did those words have to come out her mouth? I just fucking lost it. Before I knew what was happening, I slapped the shit out of Grace. I slapped her so hard she went sailing across the room.

"Get the fuck up bitch. I don't feel sorry for your trifling ass. You fucked Tony, and all this time you been smiling and shit, up in my face like ain't shit happened. Damn, Mya warned me not to bring my man around your hoe-ish ass, but naw, I didn't listen. Grace wouldn't fuck my man. That's my girl. I guess I was fucking wrong," I screamed.

"Max please!" cried Grace.

"Those tears don't mean shit to me Grace. Cry bitch, cry. Cause you got a serious ass whooping coming," I said.

I tried to stomp the shit out of Grace, but this bitch was quick on her feet. She ran into the bathroom, and locked herself in.

"Max, please, I love you, don't do this," cried Grace.

"Love? Bitch, you don't know the fucking meaning of love," I hollered.

When I tell you I was on fire, you probably could see steam rising from my head. I kept banging on the bathroom door.

"Bitch come out, and take your ass whooping like a woman since you want to fuck my ex-man. Correction, he wasn't my ex at the time, he was my man," I screamed. Silence, there was no more pleading from the other side of the door.

"Grace I know you hear me. Open the fucking door. I'm out this bitch. You can't stay locked up in the bathroom forever. I'll see you in the streets. And when I do, be ready to get your ass whooped ghetto style," I said.

"Max, please don't leave, I need you," hollered Grace.

Before I knew it, I ran back in the apartment, trying to break the bathroom door down.

"Bitch, you didn't need me, when you fucked my man," I screamed.

After hearing this shit, I knew had to go calm down. I'm not the ghetto, fighting type. But, that shit brought me back to my ghetto roots. I knew I had to get, as far away from Grace as possible. The night air would do me some good. I needed to gather my thoughts. I didn't want to do something crazy, and end up in jail. That shit ain't worth it. There was a numbness in me that I couldn't shake, right in the pit of my stomach. It felt like someone had dropped kicked me right in the gut. This was a hurt that was hitting my heart. The hurt I was feeling at that moment, seemed to be escalating. I felt like I was going crazy. I needed to talk to someone.

Without warning, the tears just started rolling down my face. Not tears of sorrow, but tears of pain. Just knowing my home-girl, fucked my man, and I didn't have a clue. Now that I think back, she used to always be saying how fine Tony was, and that I was lucky as hell to have him. But, I never thought, my girl was even looking at him that way. Grace was like a sister to me. Don't get me wrong, Tony was a dime piece, plus some. After the initial shock set in, I finally settled down. I knew my next move was to call Tony. I didn't even know how to go about approaching him with this information. Should I just go the fuck off, or slap the shit out him.

Right now, I needed to just chill. The night breeze will soothe me. I decided to relax, and drink me a glass of wine. I can vividly remember the day when I met Tony. I had got a flat tire on I-75 and Eureka Rd. I called AAA insurance. I'm standing on the side of the road, by my car, when the tow truck pulls up. Out of the truck, comes this dirty looking tow truck driver. He was looking down at his clipboard. When he looked up at me, with those bedroom eyes, and that beautiful smile, I almost melted. He was dirty as hell, but oh my, my, my, this nigga was fine, dirt and all. I just kept looking at him as if I was in a trance.

"Ms Taylor, Ms Taylor, hello did you call for service?" he asked.

"Oh, I'm sorry. I didn't hear you," I lied. He just smiled.

"You look like you were in deep thought," he said.

If he only knew my deep thought was how big his dick was, and could he fuck? I guess those thoughts came from not getting it on a regular. Ok, now I'm thinking, how can I get this man's number without looking desperate?

"It looks like you ran over a nail, Ms Taylor. Or, is that Mrs. Taylor?" he asked. There is a God.

"No, that's Ms Taylor, and your name?" I asked.

"Oh, I'm sorry, Tony, Tony Thomas," he replied.

Damn, Max Thomas sounds good. Look at me claiming him for a husband already, and just met him.

"I'll have your tire changed in no time, and have you back on the road," he smiled.

"Oh, I'm in no hurry, take your time," I said.

I had to think fast. How the hell could I give him my number? Ok, get a grip Max, think, think.

"Tony, have you had lunch yet?'

"No, why?"

"I think I owe you lunch for taking care of me," I said.

"This is part of my job; you don't have to do that," he replied.

"But, I insist."

"Ok, if you insist," he said.

"I insist. We can stop at Chili's right on Eureka Rd," I said.

"Hey, wait, I'm all greasy and dirty," said Tony looking down at his clothes.

"Don't you have an extra shirt in your truck?" I asked, smiling.

"Oh, no, I'm not going out like this," he said as he walked toward his truck.

"Hey, wait a minute; let me take you out to dinner then. I'm sorry Tony. I'm going on, and on. I never did ask if you were dating someone or if you were married," I said.

"No, to your first, and second question," he laughed.

"Well, let me give you my number. Call me when you're available," I said.

"How about tonight, if that's ok?" he asked.

"Tonight will be fine. I'll pick you up, if that's all right with you," I replied.

"I'm not used to letting the woman pick me up, why don't I pick you up?"

"Ok, it's a date. Pick me up at seven. My number is (313) 222-2555," I smiled.

Dinner was great; he was the perfect gentleman. He was what every woman, wants in a man, and some. He was Mr. Handyman, all the way around, from fixing your car, to repairing everything you could name in your house that needed to be fixed. Come to find out, he had taken a very, very early retirement from UPS as a driver. He cashed out on his 401K plan to open up a repair, and towing shop. He said he wasn't getting any younger, and he couldn't see himself delivering packages for the rest of his life. Plus it was starting to take a toll on his body. He said he was having too many aches and pains. Outside of that, he was always playing basketball on somebody's league.

He said he normally works from his home where he has an office setup. But he had a couple of workers off sick, so he filled in whenever needed to help cover. I guess you could say brother man had it going on in the legal sense. Every nigga that I had been meeting lately was in the drug game, and I was not trying to go there. I like to sleep peacefully at night without having to look over my shoulder all the time. That's what I tried telling my sister Lynn, and Mya. But they ain't trying to hear that.

Chapter – 10

Tony

Tony turned out to be a sweet heart, one-of-a-kind. I asked him why he wasn't married, or in a relationship. He said that he had gotten out of a relationship about six months ago. The woman turned out to be a gold digger, always needing something. In his words, she was just too needy. Tony was my friend, and of course, my lover. He was the first guy I had made love to that made me have multiple organisms. The man knew how to please a woman. He would start at the bottom, and work his way to the top. From sucking on my toes, to kissing my ass, he would lick every inch, of my body.

The love making, oh my, oh my, this man had me calling his name in every fucking language I could think of. Not that I knew how to speak every language, but shit, fuck it. I was speaking whatever sound came out my mouth. Ladies, you know what I'm talking about. I was probably speaking in tongues. God forgive me, for I have sinned. The kind of love making that makes your ass cry, and you don't even know the fuck why.I think he actually practiced that shit; he was just too damn good.

Shit, he had my pussy itching for the dick just from sucking a toe; he hadn't even made it to my titties, and that's my sensitive spot. Ladies, I hate to brag, but the man was blessed down below, and knew how to work the shit. You ever met a nigga, blessed down there, and have no fucking clue how to work that shit? And I'm not in the market to be schooling a nigga.

Yeah, what can I say, shit Tony turned a sister out. Had me watching X-rated movies, trying new shit. One day, I came home, this nigga surprised me. He was laying in my bed butt ass naked. He looked at me with those bedroom eyes and started stroking his shit. His dick started rising, oh my god. Damn, that shit was a turn on. I couldn't get out of my clothes fast enough. I was all over his ass. Knocked a sister right the fuck out. I was snoring and shit. I still laugh at myself whenever I think about that shit.

My mind was a thousand-miles away, thinking back to when we met. I had to re-check myself and get back to the situation at hand--checking Tony's ass for what had come to light. I still couldn't get the thought, out of my head that Grace would do something like this to me, of all people. We were like sisters, been friends since kindergarten. Luckily my relationship with Tony ended on good terms, which was good because Tony was a handy man around the house. Every time something broke down, I was picking up the phone calling Tony. Also, it was an excuse to see him. Love, is hard to forget.

He would never charge me for the repairs, so every now and then I would still cook him dinner. Like the record said, "It's, so hard to say good bye to yesterday," I sang.

Ok, let me get my thoughts together and call this man. His phone continued ringing. Maybe he's not home. Truthfully I don't know if I'm ready to confront him. Damn, he's home. When Tony picked up the phone, he immediately said "Ok Max, what's broke now?"

I could tell he was smiling just by the sound of his voice. Before I knew it, I just cut into him.

"Tell me the truth Tony, did you ever fuck Grace?" I screamed into the phone. There was silence on the phone. He just started saying, how sorry he was. This shocked the shit out of me. I thought his initial reaction would be to deny the shit, but instead he just kept saying how sorry he was. He said he was glad the truth finally came out because it was hard these last two years to look me in the face without feeling guilty.

He explained to me that he was at the club one night, and had a little too much to drink. He said that Grace offered to drive him home, but instead she took him to her house. She told him to sleep it off, and she would drop him off in the morning. He said ok, since Grace was my girl, and that I would probably be glad she looked out for her boo.

"Max, I woke up to your girl giving me mega head. I tried to push her off; my mind was telling me to stop, but my body wouldn't resist. I knew Grace was your girl, and all I could think about was how much I loved you Max. I said to myself, why is her girl Grace, doing this to me. I kept telling Grace we shouldn't be doing this," he said.

"Tony, Grace said, she fucked you," I hollered.

"Max, if giving a nigga head is her version of fucking, then she fucked my dick with her mouth. Max, I kept telling her this is wrong. She just kept saying, Max doesn't have to know. It'll be our little secret. Now you know why every time she came around I would make an excuse, and leave. I couldn't bear to be around her after that incident, knowing what we had done to you. You didn't deserve that Max," he said

"Is that why you broke it off with me?" I asked.

"Yes!"

"Now when I think back, I do recall how whenever Grace came around, you would just leave saying you had to take care of some business or something. We did break up on good terms, but that was a sorry ass excuse you gave me Tony," I said

"I know Max. I couldn't bear to go on looking at you knowing I had hurt you. You didn't deserve it. It was killing me every day, to even look you in the face knowing what had happened," he said.

Chapter – 11

Max

This time, I cried letting go pain because in my heart I still loved Tony and was hoping one day we could get back together. After hearing this, I needed to get away, and I mean far away. Not stuck in my apartment, but long distance. I needed to spend some time alone to clear my head. I called Mya, and told her everything that had happened. I already knew what she was going to say.

"Max didn't I tell your ass I didn't trust Grace. I knew some shit like this was gone happen. Trust me, I ain't surprised. I hope you gave that bitch a good old fashioned ass whooping because if you didn't, we can go over there now. You know, I got your back," said Mya.

Gwen Cannon

"Mya, I'm not trying to hear that right now, ok. I need to get away from Detroit altogether. I need to clear my head. I was thinking about Jamaica," I said.

"You know your ass ain't going to Jamaica without me. I might find me a Jamaica Mon!"

"Mya, your ass is crazy."

"See, I got you laughing already," she laughed.

"My ass gone get in trouble in another country fooling with your crazy ass," I said.

"Girl, you know you need me. Plus I need a vacation after the shit my aunt pulled. Max did you tell Lynn?" asked Mya.

"Naw, Lynn can't hold fucking water when it comes to any kind of drama, or gossip. My mother and everybody in the family would know," I replied.

• • •

We left for Jamaica that weekend. Believe the commercials, Jamaica is beautiful, and the men, oh my god. I think that their accent is what gets you. It just sounds so sensuous and sexy. Makes you want to rip your panties off. I see why Stella got her groove back. Right now, I just needed some time away, to clear my head. Get my mind off work and the drama with Tony and Grace. I'm glad our hotel was on the beach. It was a beautiful site to wake up to in the morning.

I awaked to the sun rise over a beautiful blue ocean view. I never knew water could be so blue.

"Wake up Max; it's time to go shopping," Mya pulled the covers off me.

"I knew that's why your ass wanted to come," I said.

"Ok, ok, I admit it. You know I'm a - shopaholic I'm addicted," she said.

We shopped, we ate, and we shopped some more.

"Mya, your ass is wearing me out, with all this damn shopping. I haven't even had time to think. I don't know what I'm going to do, about Grace, and Tony," I said.

"Shit, if you want my opinion, fuck both of them. I'll tell you what you need to do Max, whoop Grace's ass some more. Go home, and fuck the shit out of Tony, and then drop his ass." She started doing her booty dance.

"Oooo, you nasty. Why would I do that," I asked.

"Shit, why wouldn't you. Pay back is a monster. Your ass, know you want some more of Tony's good loving. That's why, you so uptight. You need some dick," Mya licked her top lip.

"Fuck you, Mya," I laughed.

"Oh such language mon, coming from Ms Max. Are you going to get you some Jamaican dick? That's what Stella did," said Mya.

"Don't go there bitch!" I replied.

"Know what, your ass keep saying I'm crazy. You're the crazy one. All this Jamaican dick running around and you just gone pass it up. Well, I'm taking me a souvenir back, some Jamaican dickkk." She starting dancing around the room.

"Your ass is crazzzzzzzzyyyyyy Mya. Do you really think I would fuck some stranger? I love you Mya. I'm really glad you came," I said.

"I already know that Max. I'm irresistible! Have you decided what you're going to do? We'll be home tomorrow,"

"I don't know Mya, I love Grace. Even though she broke the sister-friend code, never sleep with your sister's, or friend's man," I replied.

I had been thinking long and hard over the past few days about what happened. I know Grace is going to need family, and friends to get her through this ordeal. I can't even imagine what this is going to do to her. I'm just worried about Tony.

"Max, didn't you say, Tony said that Grace was giving him head?" asked Mya.

"Yes! I don't think you can catch AIDS from getting head. But, it's better to be safe, than sorry. Shit I know I'm going to go get myself checked when we get back home. Tony might be lying about just getting head," I said.

"I don't think he would lie to you about that. That's some serious shit. Max, you got me thinking now. Shit, is Andre straight? Brother be going downtown on a sister real strong. Max, are you scared?" she asked.

"Call it what you want, I'm getting checked. You should go with me Mya," I said. "Shit I'm straight. I use a raincoat every fucking time. Ain't no chocolate dipstick going in my honey, without being covered. Chocolate is my favorite," she starting sucking on her finger.

"Your ass is nasty," I smiled.

Chapter – 12

Grace

After my trip to Jamaica, I came back home with a new attitude. I called my mother, and father to tell them I love them and that everything was ok with me. If they don't hear from me at least once a week they go into a panic and start calling all my friends. Grace was the last person I wanted my parents to call, so I made sure to check in with them. Lynn of course was drilling me with questions and wanting answers about what was going on, and why I ran off to Jamaica. I had several messages from Grace, saying how sorry she was and I was her sister for life.

She was actually crying on the phone, saying how she really needed me to help her through the situation she was in. She kept saying that she needed someone, who understood her. I just shook my head. Grace had broken the code of faith between a sister, and friend. That's never, ever sleep with your girl's man. Don't she know that shit should be written in stone and passed as a law?

The last message brought me back out of my trance. Grace's mother was saying that she was in the hospital getting her first treatment. She said that Grace had an attack of some sort. I immediately went into friend mode, and called her mother. Even though she had done some foul shit, I still had mad love for her. Grace's mother filled me in on all the details of Grace's condition. When I got to the hospital, Grace was asleep; she looked like an angel.

I just stood there watching her and the tears started to flow. My hatred for Grace at that moment disappeared. I just wanted to tell her it was going to be alright, and that I would always have her back. When Grace woke up, I know I was the last person she expected to see sitting in her room. She just smiled and looked at me. I gave her a big bear hug, and stopped her from saying what I knew she was about to say.

"Grace, life is too short to dwell on the past. I'm here, and I'm going to see you through this. You are a fighter, so bitch start fighting before I kill your ass for real," I laughed.

All she could do was laugh.

"How in the hell did you get Mya to come with you?" she asked.

"Trust me, I practically had to pull a gun on her ass and kidnap her," I replied.

"Can I get a hug, Mya?" asked Grace.

"Grace, you lucky I love your ass," replied Mya.

"I'm so glad you came, just like old times, the awesome three," Grace smiled.

After making out a long list of men, and making numerous calls. It took about two weeks, before we actually found out who Grace contracted the disease from. It was this guy we all knew. His name was Rick. But what really got us was that this nigga knew he had the disease. To make a long story short, he didn't care who he gave the shit to. I immediately called the police to arrest his ass. This bitch ass nigga was going around basically killing people and didn't give a fuck.

My biggest fear, besides Grace having the disease was Tony. I know it was a blowjob, but better to be safe, than sorry. I hoped, and prayed he didn't have that shit. My test results came back negative. Thank God! As we waited in the doctor's office for Tony's results I told him that I still loved him, and I understood why he broke up with me. The nurse called Tony to come into the doctor's office.

"Max, I want you to come with me. I need your support, now more than ever," Tony said.

"Tony Thomas, your results came back negative," the doctor said.

I think I was more excited than Tony. We hugged for the longest. Thanking God and praising him for getting us through this. Later that night we had a long talk. I told Tony that I wanted to take it slow, take one day at a time.

"I understand Max. I just couldn't face you, knowing what took place. You just don't know how much I missed you," he hugged me tightly.

Chapter – 13

Lynn

My niece is now two years old, and I have the utmost respect for Corey. I don't even call him the N word. It just don't feel right. He has nothing but love for Lynn and his baby girl. But Lynn don't appreciate a real man. She wants a damn baller. I can tell by her actions. Whenever this nigga we grew up with named Chico walks by, she is all smiles and shit. "Damn, the nigga ok, but that's about it. Money ain't everything. You have a good ass man at home, so you need to get your priorities straight," I said.

"I don't know Max, he just does something to me every time I see him with his fine, sexy ass," said Lynn.

"Lynn, you don't want to be looking over your shoulder every time you with a nigga like that," I said.

I told her ass she was just like my girl Mya, in so many ways. I don't know what it is about a thuggish nigga. Stop looking at the money. It might look good now, but that shit can kill you.

"You, Mya, and Grace. Oh, sorry. I can't throw Grace in that group. She just fucks for free. Never come up with any money!" I said. "Max, your girl got that reputation put on herself. She's a big ass hoe," said Lynn loudly.

"Don't say that about her Lynn," I said.

"You be saying it, why I can't?" she asked.

"I know, but that's still my girl. Promise me Lynn, you won't be with no drug dealer. You got a good ass man," I said.

I experienced that drug dealer's woman shit; didn't like it. Too much pressure wondering what might happen next.

"Max, Corey surprised me with a trip to the Bahamas. We're, leaving tomorrow," she said.

"Can I go?"

"No!"

"Why, I won't be with y'all. You and Corey always going to some damn island," I said.

"I know, I told him let's go to Vegas or maybe New York. I can go shopping in New York. I gotta go Max, I have to pack," said Lynn as she was going out the door.

"Damn, your ass hasn't packed yet?"I shouted.

"Corey, hurry up, were going to miss our flight," said Lynn.

"I'm coming Lynn, I have to grab something from my office. Damn, I hate flying," he said.

"I'm going to have me a glass of wine, and go to sleep," said Lynn.

"Ok, I'll wake you up when we're about to land. Damn, this is a smooth flight. I guess, I can catch up on some work. I'm glad, I brought my laptop. Lynn, baby, wake up, we're about to land," He said.

"Damn, it seems like we got here fast," replied Lynn.

"When we check into the hotel, I have to make a run,"

"Damn, Corey, we just got here. Who the fuck do you know in the Bahamas?"

"Lynn, shut the fuck up."

"Who the fuck do you think you are talking to?" shouted Lynn.

"I got a lot on my mind. Please, just stop with the fifty questions," he said.

"Ok, just remember who the fuck, you're talking to. I'm not one of your ex hoes," replied Lynn.

"Know what? I don't have time for this. I'll see you later," said Corey.

I must have really been tired from the flight. I fall asleep in my clothes. It's two in the morning, and where the fuck is Corey at? I decided to go out on the beach it looked so relaxing. As I was approaching the beach, I could have sworn I heard Corey's voice. I stopped to listen. It was Corey, he was arguing with some foreign man. I could see the man had expensive tastes because I know clothes, and the suit he had on must have cost no less than a grand. What in the fuck could Corey and this man be arguing over. Shit, Corey told me he had never been to the Bahamas. Bam, Bam! What the fuck! Corey, shot the man.

"Corey, what the fuck are you doing? screamed Lynn.

"Lynn, what the fuck are you doing out here?" asked Corey.

"Uhhh I was going to take a walk on the beach," said Lynn.

"Lynn, what the fuck are you doing on the beach? It's after two in the morning," said Corey.

This pretty bohemian woman comes up behind me.

"Corey, do you know this woman?" asked the bohemian woman.

"God damn Lynn, why the fuck did you have to see this," said Corey.

"What, see you shoot somebody? Will you please tell me what the fuck is going on," shouted Lynn.

"Corey, who is this broad?" Lynn demanded.

"Corey, you didn't tell me you were bringing your hoe from the states," said the bohemian woman.

"Hoe? Who the fuck do you think you're talking to? You bohemian bitch. I will whoop your ass like I'm your momma and put you to fucking bed," shouted Lynn.

"We have to get rid of her Corey," said the bohemian.

"We ain't getting rid of shit, that's my daughter's mother. She'll keep quiet. Won't you Lynn?" said Corey.

By now, I didn't know what the fuck to do, but go along. Who was this man I thought I knew. "Lynn, baby, don't look shocked, how the fuck you think you got that hundred grand? I don't make that type of money. I make decent money, but not that much," explained Corey. "Corey, I want to go home, now!" screamed Lynn.

"You ain't going no damn where until I say so," said Corey.

"Bam, Bam! Oh, what the fuck, Corey are you crazy?" asked Lynn.

"I had to kill her; she was going to kill you. I couldn't let that happen. Well Lynn, now you know," said Corey.

"Know what? That you are a fucking killer, and a drug dealer," replied Lynn.

"Yeah, I guess you can say both. This transaction went bad. This nigga tried to play me. Shit, I didn't come all this way for nothing. It was either him or me," said Corey.

"And the bitch Corey, who was she? Your island hoe?" said Lynn.

"She was my inside connect. See, I can double for my money here," said Corey.

"Corey, you're talking to me, like I'm alright with this shit. Please don't get it twisted," said Lynn.

Smack!

Gwen Cannon

"What the fuck, no you didn't hit me," screamed Lynn.

"There's more, where that came from if you don't shut the fuck up Lynn. I'm trying to think," said Corey.

"All I know is, I want you to take me the fuck home now," said Lynn, as the tears started to fall.

"You money, hungry bitch. Now, you want to jump ship, and run your ass home. Sorry baby girl, you're in this for the long haul," he said dragging her down the beach.

"What the fuck, do you mean by that Corey? asked Lynn.

"Were, going to get married," said Corey.

"Hell naw!" shouted Lynn.

"Oh, hell yes! If you want to keep on living, we're getting married," said Corey.

"So if I don't. You gone kill me?" replied Lynn.

"You said it, I didn't," said Corey.

"I must be fucking dreaming," said Lynn.

"No, it ain't a dream baby girl. I don't think I can trust your ass, not after this Lynn. If you so much as think about telling anybody. Just remember what you saw here. Don't you love our daughter?" said Corey.

"I know you wouldn't harm our daughter," said Lynn.

"That's my baby, I would never hurt her. But you, you're just a money hungry bitch," he laughed.

All the words Max kept telling me started ringing in my head. Don't date a drug dealer. But how the fuck did I know Corey was one with his innocent, looking ass.

I couldn't wait to touch U.S. soil. We hardly spoke on the flight home. I was too fucking scared to say anything. Now, I just had to play along with whatever game Corey was playing.

Chapter -14

Lynn

"Max, did you know Corey proposed to Lynn?" asked Mya. "When?"

"Today!"

"Oh my god, my baby sister is making it to the altar before me. I'm so happy for you little sis. This is just what you need to settle your wild ass down. Lynn, why are you looking so down? You should be happy," I said.

"I'm straight, just tired from the flight," replied Lynn.

"You got to slow your ass down now, Ms Homemaker," I laughed.

"A ring on my finger, don't tame a beast," replied Lynn.

I knew I had to play this shit off. I couldn't let Max know what was really going on.

"Lynn, you need to chill out and grow the fuck up. This man has proposed to you, with his undying love, and you up here saying some foul ass shit like that," I said.

If my big sister only knew.

"Damn big sis, calm the fuck down. I was just joking," smiled Lynn.

"Yeah right, I know you Lynn. Lynn please understand when I say every woman wishes she could have a decent man like Corey," I said.

I just wanted to scream, he's a fucking drug dealer Max.

"Lynn, is it true? Corey's going to have a house built from the ground for you and Gina?" I said.

"Yes, it's true Max,"

"Lynn, I am so excited for you. We need to start making plans for the wedding, E especially if we have to make it happen in three weeks. Corey couldn't wait, he wants you to be Mrs. Smith in three weeks," I said. Corey gave Lynn a spending limit of fifteen thousand dollars. I was like goddamn; he really loves my little sister. For someone who was getting married in three weeks, my sister did not look like the happy blushing bride. I tried talking to

Lynn, but she kept telling me everything was ok.

Lynn took advantage of the fifteen thousand dollars. I probably would have told Corey, we'll spend five thousand on the wedding. And put the rest toward things for the new house. Oh no, not my sister, she only wanted the best, because she thought she was the best.

"So who's going to be your maid of honor, and how many brides maids? I asked.

"Now Max, you already know, don't be standing there smiling and shit. You know it's you, my one and only sister. I guess Grace, and Mya will be bride's maids. You know, I can count on one hand my females friends," said Lynn.

"Maybe it's you with your 'I am queen bee' attitude that chases a lot of females away from you Lynn," I said.

"I can't help it. If I was blessed with beauty, and a booty," replied Lynn.

"You are crazy, little sis. Too bad you weren't blessed with brains to go with it," I said.

"What did you say Max? asked Lynn, while turning up her nose.

"Nothing, Lynn,"

"Max don't hate,"

"Ok, earth to Lynn, earth to Lynn; please snap back to reality. You ain't all that! You have beauty on the outside, but your attitude is fucked up little sister. I don't know how I put up with your high and mighty ass," I said, twirling my neck.

"Because you love me, and I'm your only sister," replied Lynn.

"Yeah I guess that's it," I said

• • •

Three weeks rolled around very fast. It was the day before the wedding. We decided to take Lynn out to the club instead of throwing her a bachelorette party, since she didn't have any friends anyway.

I didn't feel like seeing, a naked ass man all up in my face. My hormones were already in high gear from being sex starved too long. The club was packed as usual. I told Grace to tell Mya, to meet us at 7:00 p.m. That way, she would get there by 9:00 p.m., with her slow ass.

Lynn was having a good time telling everyone that she would be a married woman by this time tomorrow. But, there was still something not right about Lynn. I couldn't put my finger on it. All the so-called ballers were buying her drinks, and wishing her good luck.

"Lynn slow the fuck down on the drinks. You have to be up by 6:00 a.m. to get your hair and nails done," I said.

"I know big sister, I'm straight," replied Lynn.

"Ask Grace and Mya. Right Mya? Right Grace? Don't I look like I'm straight," slurred Lynn.

"I don't know. Your sister may be right, you look a little tipsy Lynn," said Grace.

"I'm ok!" Lynn shouted loudly.

"That's what your mouth is saying, but your body is saying, I want to go to sleep," said Grace.

At 1:00 a.m. I told Lynn let's go.

"Maybe she ain't ready to leave yet," said Chico.

"Chico, where did you come from?" I asked. "I've been watching your sister from across the dance floor. I don't think she's finished celebrating her last day being a single woman," said Chico, while handing her another drink.

"Max, I'm straight," said Lynn.

"Lynn, you're drunk," I shouted.

"Chico, Chico, let's dance," said Lynn. "Naw, I don't think Max would like that. She's been grimming me all night. I don't know why she don't like me. Lynn, I can take you home if you want me to," said Chico.

"Yeah, that sounds good," replied Lynn.

"Naw, Chico I got her," I said.

"Max, I wouldn't let anything happen to your sister," said Chico.

"Yeah Max, he wouldn't let anything happen to me. 'I'm a grown ass woman," said Lynn.

I saw Lynn whispering something in Chico's ear. He was just smiling, saying all right, bet. I told Mya, and Grace that I was taking Lynn home.

"I'll be right back ladies. My sister is drunk," I said. Damn, finally made it home.

"Lynn, take your ass straight to bed, and I will pick you up at 5:30 a.m. We have to get your hair and nails done in the morning," I said as I kissed her on the cheek.

"Ok big sister, see you later. Luv ya!" replied Lynn.

"Luv you, too," I said.

When I got back to the club, Mya, and Grace ran up to me.

"Max, Chico was bragging to his boys how he was about to go, and tear Lynn's pussy up," said Grace.

I ran straight to the parking lot looking for Chico.

"Hey Andre, you seen Chico?" I asked.

"Yeah, he just pulled off about ten minutes ago," said Andre.

By the time I got to Lynn's house, I could tell something wasn't right. The front door was open, and the house was dark. I started turning on lights. I called out Lynn's name, no answer.

"Lynn, where are you?" I said.

Still no answer. As I approached the door to her bedroom, all I could see was red. There was blood everywhere. I saw Lynn on the bed, she wasn't moving. Someone had shot my little sister point blank in the face, I couldn't even recognize her. A piece of paper was on her chest, it read. *"All money hungry bitches always die."*

Chapter 15

Lynn

The news of Lynn's murder, spread throughout the community. Everyone was calling me, telling me how sorry they were, and to give my family their blessings, and prayers. The funeral was standing room only. I didn't realize so many people liked my sister. I almost lost it, when Chico came up to me, and tried to hug me. He wanted to give me his condolences.

"Motherfucker you killed my sister," I screamed.

"Max, please it wasn't me, believe me," said Chico.

"Believe you, your bitch ass was going around bragging about tearing her pussy up at the club to your boys," I said.

"Max, I didn't do this shit! Please, let me talk to you in private," said Chico.

"Calm down Max, don't do this shit at your sister's funeral. There's a time and place for everything," said Mya.

"Mya, you don't understand, that was my little sister. I was, supposed to protect her," I said, sobbing uncontrollably.

I went to the ladies room, and put some cold water on my face. I have to get my thoughts straight, if I want to find out who did this shit. I decided to listen to what Chico had to say. I called Chico later that day, and asked him to meet me at Chili's.

"Max, I did go by your sister's house that night at the club. I left right behind you. I pulled over, and waited for you to leave. Before I could get out of my car, Corey pulls up, and goes into the house. The next thing I know, I hear gun shots, and Corey came running out. I immediately pulled off," said Chico.

"Why didn't you say something Chico?" I asked.

"Shit, I knew, I would be blamed for this shit. Look how you reacted, when I came into the church. I had to pay my respects," replied Chico.

"So you're telling me that Corey, her daughter's father shot and killed my sister the day before their wedding," I said.

"Yes Max, if you want me to, I'll go to the police. This shit has been hanging over my head for the last few days. My conscience is tearing me up. Believe it, or not, I really liked your sister; she had class. I admit, I'm a drug dealer Max, not a murderer," Said Chico.

"Ok, Chico, before we go to the police, I want to do something first," I said.

"Max don't go and do some crazy shit like try and kill the nigga yourself," said Chico.

For a whole week, I was in a trance. I still couldn't believe that Corey would kill my sister. I knew she had done some foul shit, while they were together. But, to just kill her. It ain't worth it, let the shit die. I decided to go see Corey.

"Hey Corey, how's my little niece doing?" I asked.

"She's ok, I have to pick her up from your mom's. Max, I didn't know you were coming over, you should have called first," said Corey.

"Oh, I didn't know you wanted me to start calling, I normally just come over. Do you have company, or something?" I asked.

"Corey, Corey, are you ready yet?" A woman's voice said.

"Who's that calling you Corey?" I asked.

"Oh, that's my cousin, she just came in from Atlanta," replied Corey.

"Oh, tell her to come on out so I can meet her," I said.

"I think she's getting dressed," said Corey. "Where's Gina?" I asked as I was looking him up, and down.

"I told you, at your mother's. I'm going to pick her up in about an hour," replied Corey.

"Hey Corey, I didn't hear the doorbell. Hi, I'm Liz, Corey's friend," Said Liz.

"Friend, Corey told me you were his cousin from Atlanta," I said.

"Really, oh then I'm his cousin from Atlanta, if that's what he wants me to be," replied Liz, while smiling.

"Ok, Corey, what's going on? Who is Liz? And don't come with that cousin shit," I said.

"Max, Liz was my high school sweetheart. She was in town, and we went out for drinks," said Corey.

"Corey how long have you and Liz been seeing each other?" I asked.

"Were not seeing each other Max," replied Corey.

"Ok, you went out for drinks, and she just ended up spending the night? That's bullshit Corey. It ain't even been a month and you all laid up with some broad. Corey you're a grown ass man, you can admit how long you've been seeing Liz. My sister isn't alive to speak for herself," I said.

"I can answer that," said Liz.

"Ok Liz, go ahead," I said.

"Liz, just shut the fuck up," said Corey.

"Who are you telling to shut the fuck? I'm not your baby's momma," replied Liz.

"Oh Bitch, leave my sister out of this. Corey, what's going on? Rumor is, that someone saw you the night Lynn was murdered coming out of her house," I said.

Corey broke out in a sweat. He was trembling, and just started crying.

"I tried to tell your sister to shut her fucking mouth," said Corey.

"What the fuck are you talking about Corey?" I asked.

"She kept threatening me, that she was going to go to the Feds," said Corey.

"Go to the Feds about what?" I screamed.

"My personal dealings," said Corey.

"Corey, I am fucking lost. What the fuck are you talking about? Oh, my God, please tell me it isn't true Corey. Please tell me, you didn't kill my sister," I screamed.

"Lynn was your sister? asked Liz.

"Yes Liz. Didn't Corey tell you that they were getting married the day before she was killed," I said.

"No! He told me, that he was leaving his daughter's mother because she wasn't nothing but a money hungry bitch," replied Liz.

Those words she said, confirmed what I had come to find out. The tears started rolling down my face. I wanted to beat the shit out of Corey.

"How could you look my family in the face knowing you had killed my sister?" I said.

"I'm so sorry Max. She didn't appreciate a good, hard working man," said Corey.

"What the fuck do you mean a good, hard working man? You son of a bitch, you killed my sister?" I screamed as the tears, started rolling down my cheeks.

"The things she would say to me Max," said Corey.

"I don't give a fuck what she said to you, she didn't deserve to die. She was the mother of your child. Didn't you think about that?" I asked.

"She didn't care about me. Lynn only cared about Lynn," said Corey.

Before I knew it, Corey took off running up the stairs. The next sound, I heard, was one gun shot, and a thud. Oh my God, please tell me he didn't shoot himself. Corey died from a self-inflicted gunshot wound to the head. My mother and father were in a state of shock. They could not believe Corey had murdered Lynn. I knew I had to be strong for Gina. She's going to need plenty of counseling. She's lost her mother, and father. All I could think about was I talked Lynn into giving Corey her phone number. I guess I can take a lesson from my own words that I'm always telling everyone. *"Everything that looks good, ain't good for you."*

Corey was a well-dressed good-looking businessman, but he had mental issues no one knew about.

We didn't attend Corey's funeral. I couldn't bring myself to attend the funeral of the man who murdered my sister. Lynn's death put a whole new outlook on life for me. It made me look at life as a blessing. It was a blessing to wake up every day, feeling healthy and strong. It was a blessing to have friends and family around you, who you love, and trust.

Gwen Cannon

I understand now, that life is what you make of it, good or bad. You have to be in control of your future. I know I have to be strong for my mother and father. I'm their only living child, and Gina will fill that emptiness of Lynn being gone. I don't think I would have made it through all of this, without Tony by my side.

He would come by every day, to make sure I was all right. I will never forget those words of warmth he said when I felt there was nothing to live for.

"Max, always remember God has a plan for everyone. God only knows why Lynn was taken away. We have to trust in him. When you get down on your knees and pray, trust me he hears your prayers," said Tony.

Those are the words I needed to hear. I look at life as being blessed.

Chapter – 16

Grace

Grace was admitted back into the hospital, after Lynn's funeral. She was being discharged today. Me and Tony decided to pick her up. She looked good, and strong. I guess the Chemotherapy treatments were working. She had lost all her hair. She refused to wear a wig, but she looked cute with her bald head and big earrings on.

"Max, I'm going to take one day at a time. I know with family and friends like you I can make it. I love you Max!" said Grace.

"I love you too, Grace," I said.

Grace told me that Mr. Fine Ass called, and cussed her out. He was one of the unlucky ones, his results were positive.

Mr. Fine, had left her a message on her answering machine the same day I had saw him at the mall? This motherfucker had the nerve to say I was trying to hit up on him. Niggas really be tripping. Grace said the message didn't even faze her, because she knew her girl too well.

We talked for the longest that day, about everything; from how we met, up to the point about her and Tony. I told Grace I love her, but with time, God heals all wounds. This nigga, Rick, is going around passing this deadly virus that kills. He's basically walking around with a loaded pistol that's going to kill everybody who gets in contact with it.

I told Grace that's attempted murder. I hope the police picked his ass up by now. Come to find out, this nigga, Rick, had all kinds of warrants: possession of marijuana, credit card theft, and stealing cars. I told Grace what was going on. My girl was in another time zone. All she kept saying was I'm going to die because of this sorry ass nigga. I wanted to tell her I told your ass to stop sleeping with every nigga you meet. I told Grace over, and over again to always use protection. But she was looking so depressed I couldn't even go there.

Grace changed after finding out she was HIV positive. It was like she was a different person. She would just keep repeating the same thing over, and over again.

"If I ever come across that motherfucker, he's dead. Not from AIDS, but from this hard ass piece of steel in my purse," she said. "Grace, are you telling me you got a gun? Please tell me no!" I asked.

"This is for protection, Max. HIV is a weapon in itself, it kills. So I need to destroy it any way I can, and if that means taking a nigga out, oh well," she said with a crazed look in her eyes.

"Grace, quit talking crazy. Grace, are you listening to me," I said.

She just looked at me as if I wasn't even there. But she didn't have to keep her word-- someone else took care of that. It was Monday night. I was looking at the 11:00 o'clock news. Rick's picture came across the TV screen stating that an unknown female shot him to death at Club Red. All I could say was please tell me it was not Grace. I immediately called her. She answered on the first ring.

"What's up girl?" said Grace.

I hadn't heard her sound this happy in a long time.

"Grace, please tell me you didn't do it," I asked.

"What?" said Grace.

"Kill that sorry ass motherfucker!" I said. "Hell naw, Max it wasn't me. But don't think for one minute if I would have seen him I would have hesitated to pull the trigger," said Grace.

Come to find out, he had given another female HIV named Eve. The report stated that, she walked into the club, and just starting shooting. He was pronounced dead, en-route to the hospital.

Chapter - 17

It's been two years, and Grace is doing well with her treatments. She went back to school, and her graduation ceremony is next month. I am so happy for my girl. I've since, opened up my own shoe store, and Tony is my Mr. Handyman. Mya, believe it or not, got pregnant (didn't use a raincoat.) Andre is the daddy. She's walking around with this big ass rock on her finger, smiling and shit. I'm going to take it slow, and maybe, just maybe I'll let Tony see what he's been missing. But believe me ladies protect yourself. Life is too short to take chances. Get to know who you are dealing with.

I don't want to make the same mistake my girl Grace made. She will be paying for her mistake for the rest of her life. Just because a nigga is fine and looks like he may have mega paper, doesn't mean he couldn't turn out to be a killer in disguise. Not a killer with a gun, but a carrier of a killer disease that will take your life in a heartbeat. Like I said, Grace was my girl. The moral of this story is, *Everything that looks good, 99% of the time ain't good for you.* Stop looking at what's on the outside. Get to know a person mentally, emotionally, and **LAST, BUT NOT LEAST, PHYSICALLY.**

About the Author

Gwen Cannon is a native of Detroit, Michigan. She currently resides in Brownstown Twp, Michigan. She was educated in the Detroit Public School System. She earned a Bachelor's degree in Business Management from Cornerstone University and is currently working on her MBA Degree in Human Resource Management.

Gwen is employed as a Release Analyst with Renaissance Global Logistics. During her spare time she loves to read, cook, write poetry and play Co-ed softball. She was so intrigued with reading various novels that it inspired her to write one herself. Although "Everything that Looks Good Ain't Good for You" is a work of fiction, much of the content was inspired from Gwen's upbringing in the Jefferies Housing

Project in Detroit, Michigan and other personal experiences. She is happily married to her soul mate James Cannon, and they have five sons, James Jr., Corey, Jonathan, Jordan, and Jalen, and one granddaughter, Co'Mya.

Coming Soon

Stuck in the dark!